[redacted]

[redacted]

TRANSFORMERS: REVENGE OF THE FALLEN
ISSUE NUMBER ONE (OF FOUR)

WRITTEN BY: **SIMON FURMAN**
PENCILS BY: **JON DAVIS-HUNT**
COLORS BY: **KRIS CARTER AND JOSH PEREZ**
LETTERS BY: **CHRIS MOWRY**
EDITS BY: **DENTON J. TIPTON**
ADAPTED FROM THE SCREENPLAY BY: **ROBERTO ORCI, ALEX KURTZMAN, AND EHREN KRUGER**

Special thanks to Hasbro's Aaron Archer, Michael Kelly, Amie Lozanzki, Va Roca, Ed Lane, Michael Provost, Erin Hillman, Samantha Lomow, and Michael Verecchia for their invaluable assistance.

To discuss this issue of *Transformers*, join the IDW Insiders, or
to check out exclusive Web offers, check out our site:

Licensed by:

www.**IDWPUBLISHING**.com

VISIT US AT
www.abdopublishing.com

Reinforced library bound edition published in 2010 by Spotlight, a division of the ABDO Group, 8000 West 78th Street, Edina, Minnesota 55439. Published by agreement with IDW Publishing. www.idwpublishing.com

Printed in the United States of America, Melrose Park, Illinois.
102009
012010

 PRINTED ON RECYCLED PAPER

Library of Congress Cataloging-in-Publication Data

Furman, Simon.
  Transformers : revenge of the fallen / written by Simon Furman ; pencils by Jon Davis-Hunt
  colors by Kris Carter and Josh Perez ; letters by Chris Mowry ; adapted from the screenplay
  by Roberto Orci, Alex Kurtzman, and Ehren Kruger.
      v. cm.
  ISBN 978-1-59961-726-8 (vol. 1) -- ISBN 978-1-59961-727-5 (vol. 2)
  ISBN 978-1-59961-728-2 (vol. 3) -- ISBN 978-1-59961-729-9 (vol. 4)
  1. Graphic novels. I. Davis-Hunt, Jon. II. Orci, Roberto. III. Kurtzman, Alex. IV. Kruger, Ehren,
  1972- V. Transformers, revenge of the fallen (Motion picture) VI. Title.
  PZ7.7.F87Tr 2010
  741.5'973--dc22

                              2009037024

All Spotlight books have reinforced library bindings and
are manufactured in the United States of America.

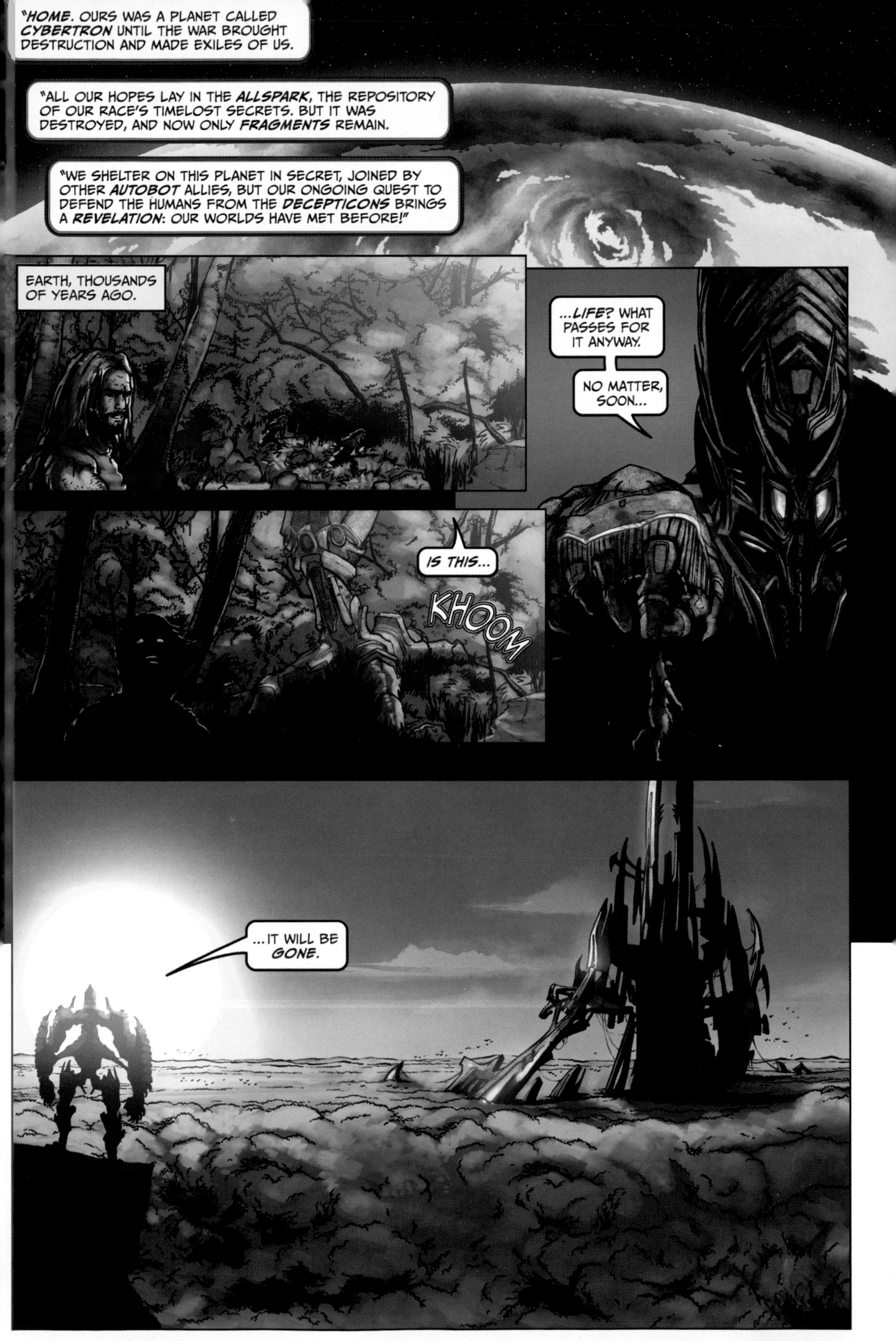
"HOME. OURS WAS A PLANET CALLED CYBERTRON UNTIL THE WAR BROUGHT DESTRUCTION AND MADE EXILES OF US.
"ALL OUR HOPES LAY IN THE ALLSPARK, THE REPOSITORY OF OUR RACE'S TIMELOST SECRETS. BUT IT WAS DESTROYED, AND NOW ONLY FRAGMENTS REMAIN.
"WE SHELTER ON THIS PLANET IN SECRET, JOINED BY OTHER AUTOBOT ALLIES, BUT OUR ONGOING QUEST TO DEFEND THE HUMANS FROM THE DECEPTICONS BRINGS A REVELATION: OUR WORLDS HAVE MET BEFORE!"
EARTH, THOUSANDS OF YEARS AGO.
IS THIS...
KHOOM
...LIFE? WHAT PASSES FOR IT ANYWAY.
NO MATTER, SOON...
...IT WILL BE GONE.

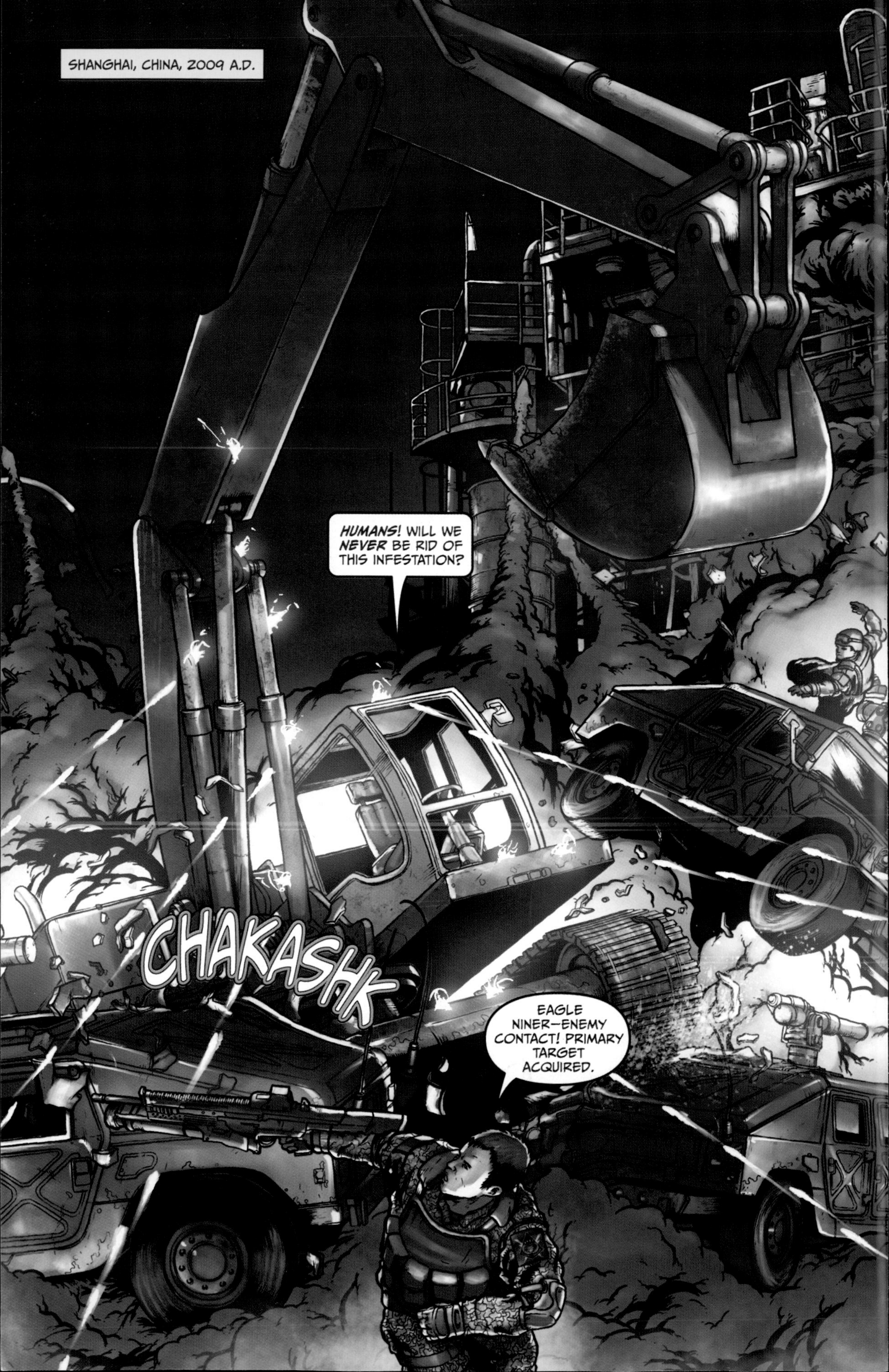
SHANGHAI, CHINA, 2009 A.D.
HUMANS! WILL WE NEVER BE RID OF THIS INFESTATION?
CHAKASHK
EAGLE NINER—ENEMY CONTACT! PRIMARY TARGET ACQUIRED.

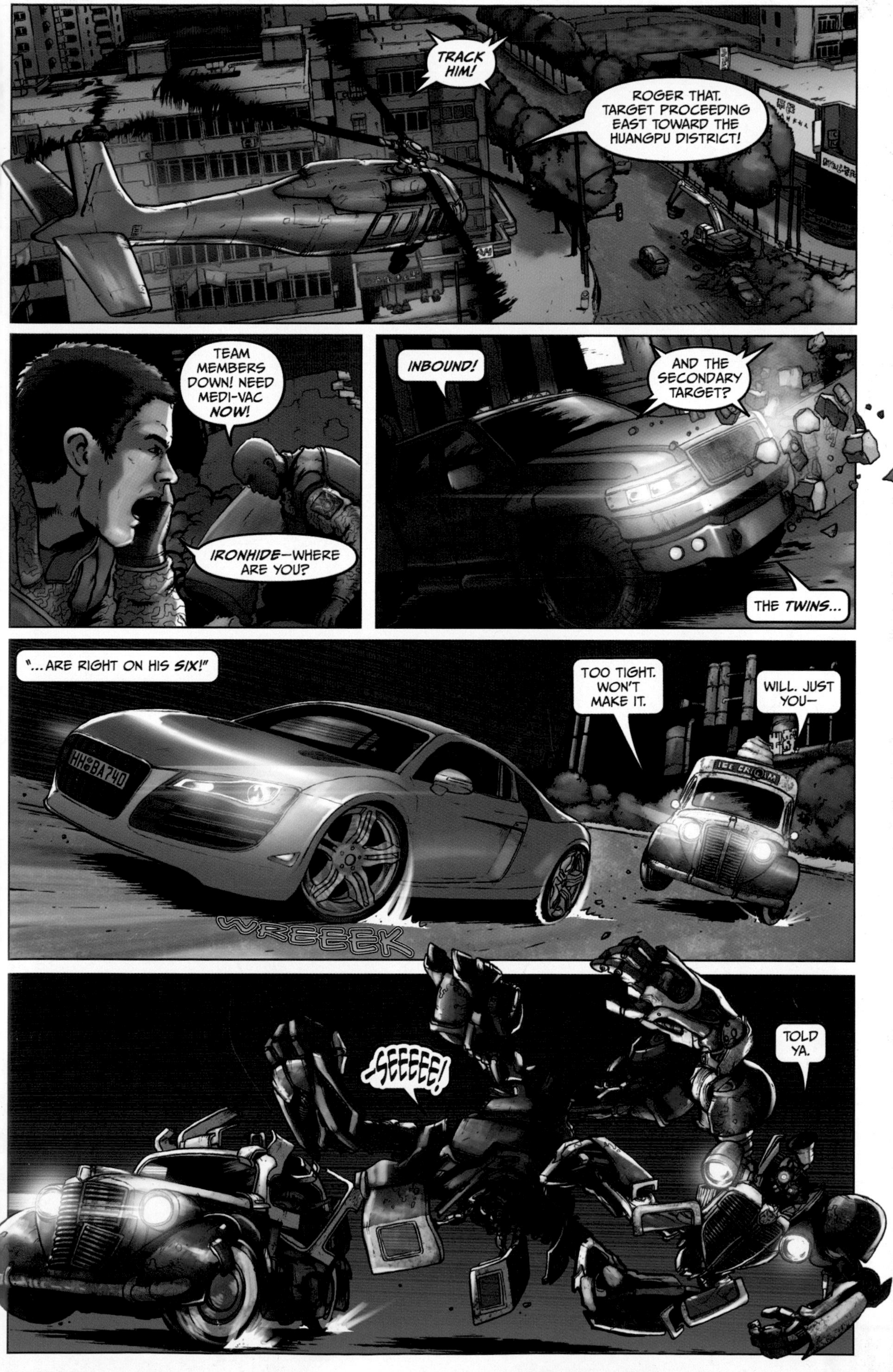
TRACK HIM!
ROGER THAT. TARGET PROCEEDING EAST TOWARD THE HUANGPU DISTRICT!
TEAM MEMBERS DOWN! NEED MEDI-VAC NOW!
IRONHIDE—WHERE ARE YOU?
INBOUND!
AND THE SECONDARY TARGET?
THE TWINS...
"...ARE RIGHT ON HIS SIX!"
TOO TIGHT. WON'T MAKE IT.
WILL. JUST YOU—
WREEEK
-SEEEEE!
TOLD YA.

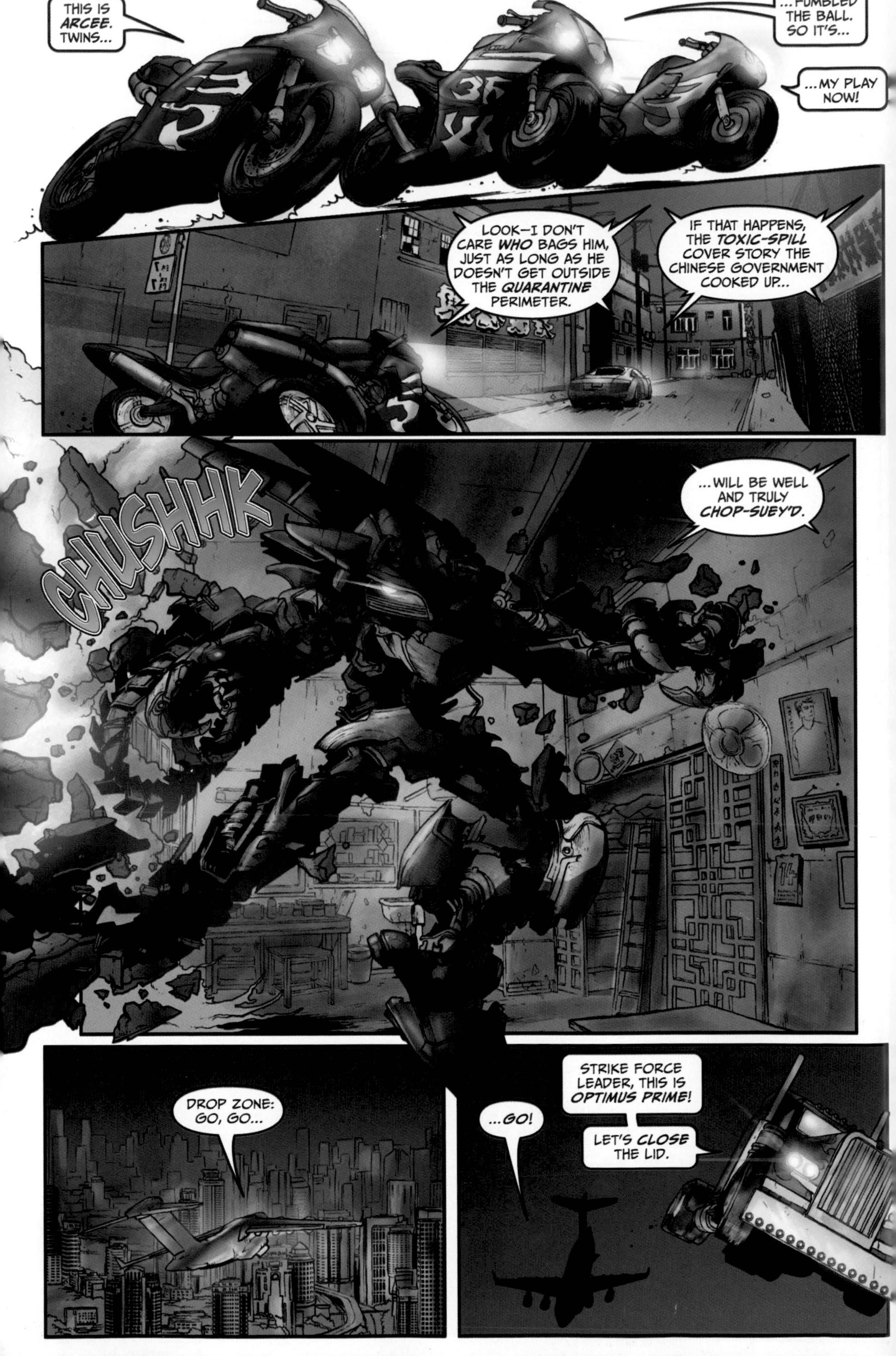
THIS IS ARCEE. TWINS...
...FUMBLED THE BALL. SO IT'S...
...MY PLAY NOW!
LOOK—I DON'T CARE WHO BAGS HIM, JUST AS LONG AS HE DOESN'T GET OUTSIDE THE QUARANTINE PERIMETER.
IF THAT HAPPENS, THE TOXIC-SPILL COVER STORY THE CHINESE GOVERNMENT COOKED UP...
CHUSHHK
...WILL BE WELL AND TRULY CHOP-SUEY'D.
DROP ZONE: GO, GO...
...GO!
STRIKE FORCE LEADER, THIS IS OPTIMUS PRIME!
LET'S CLOSE THE LID.

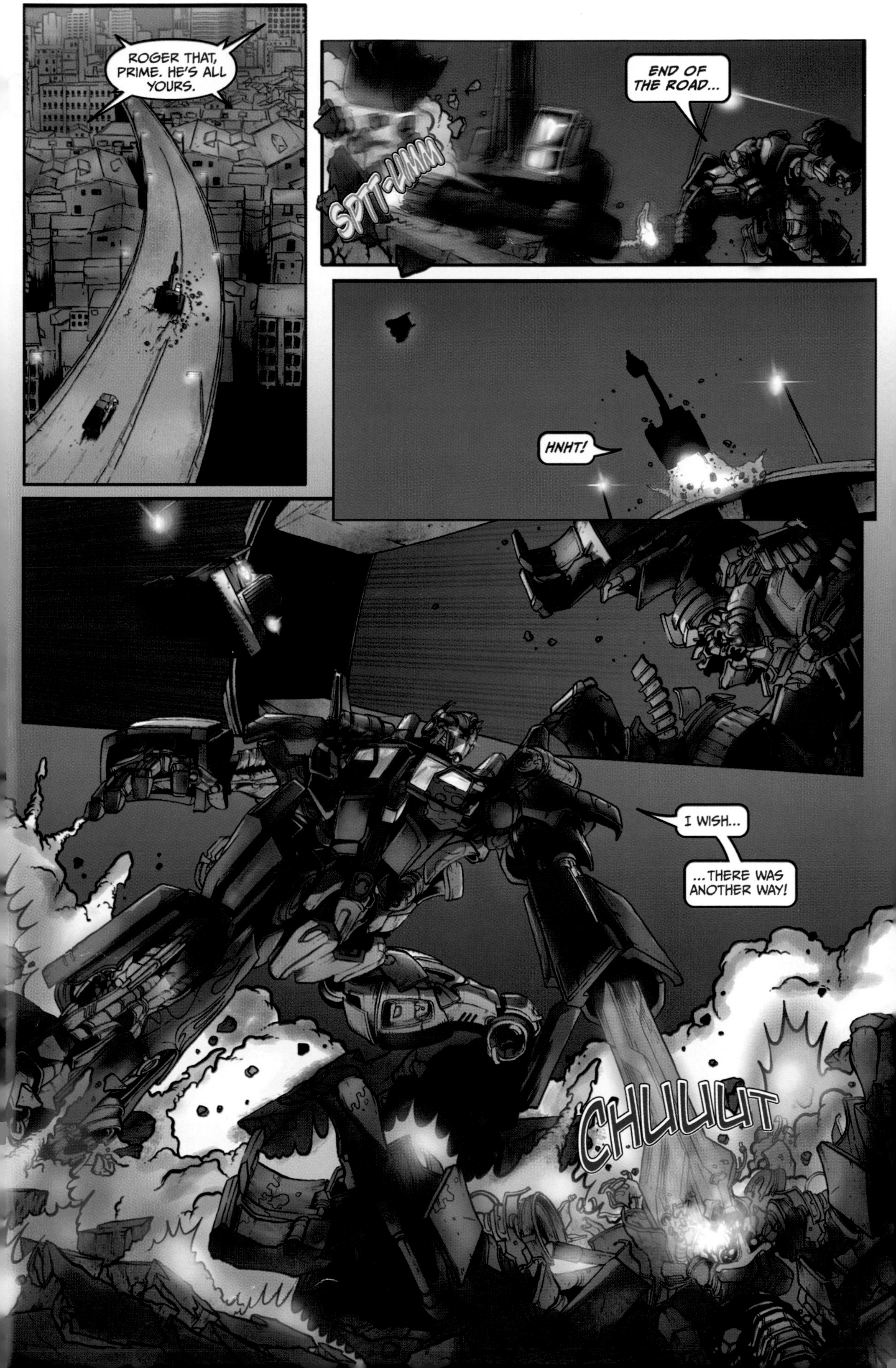
ROGER THAT, PRIME. HE'S ALL YOURS.
END OF THE ROAD...
SPTT-UMM
HNHT!
I WISH...
...THERE WAS ANOTHER WAY!
CHUUUT

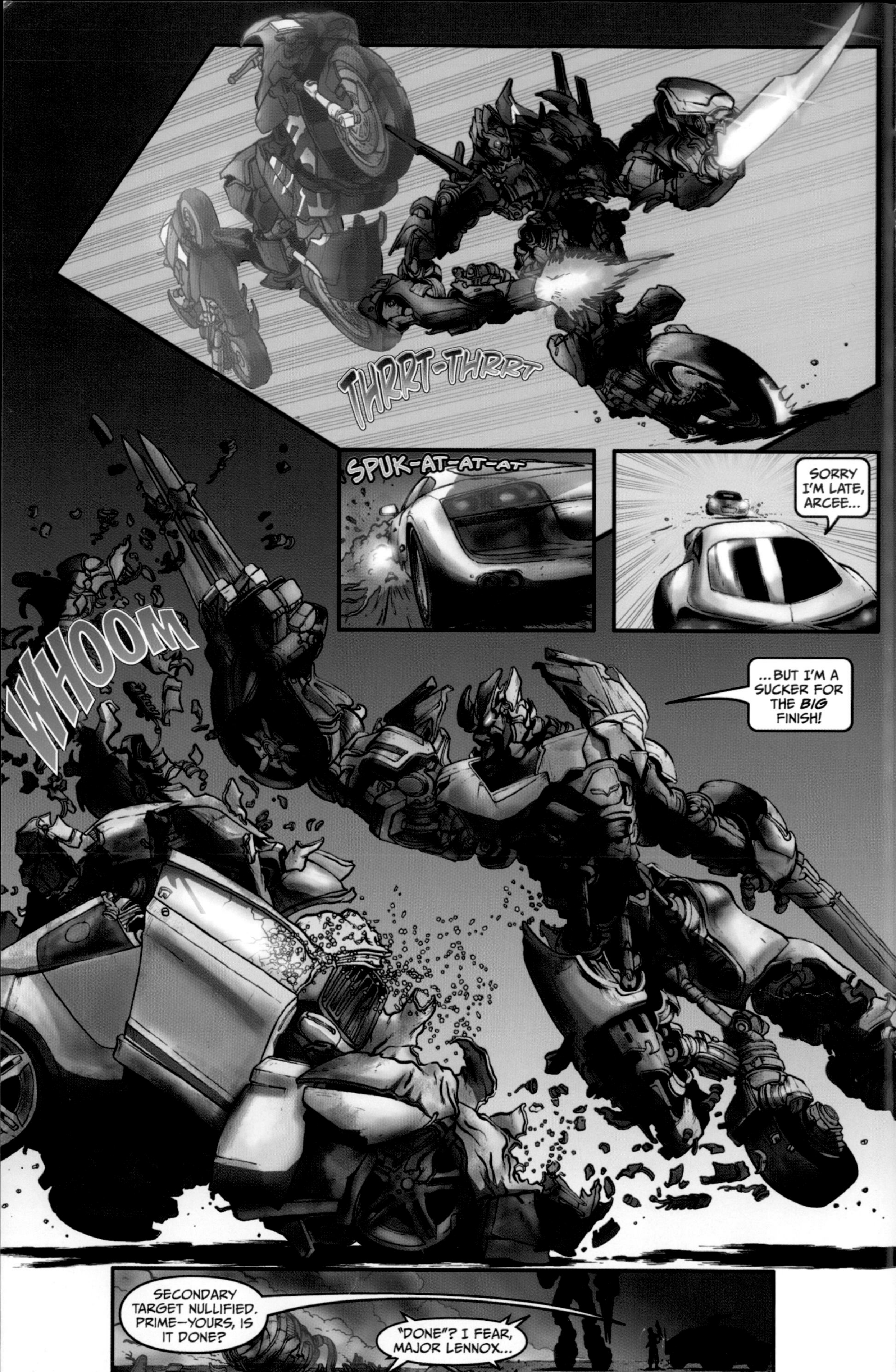
THRRT-THRRT
SPUK-AT-AT-AT
SORRY I'M LATE, ARCEE...
WHOOM
...BUT I'M A SUCKER FOR THE BIG FINISH!
SECONDARY TARGET NULLIFIED. PRIME—YOURS, IS IT DONE?
"DONE"? I FEAR, MAJOR LENNOX...

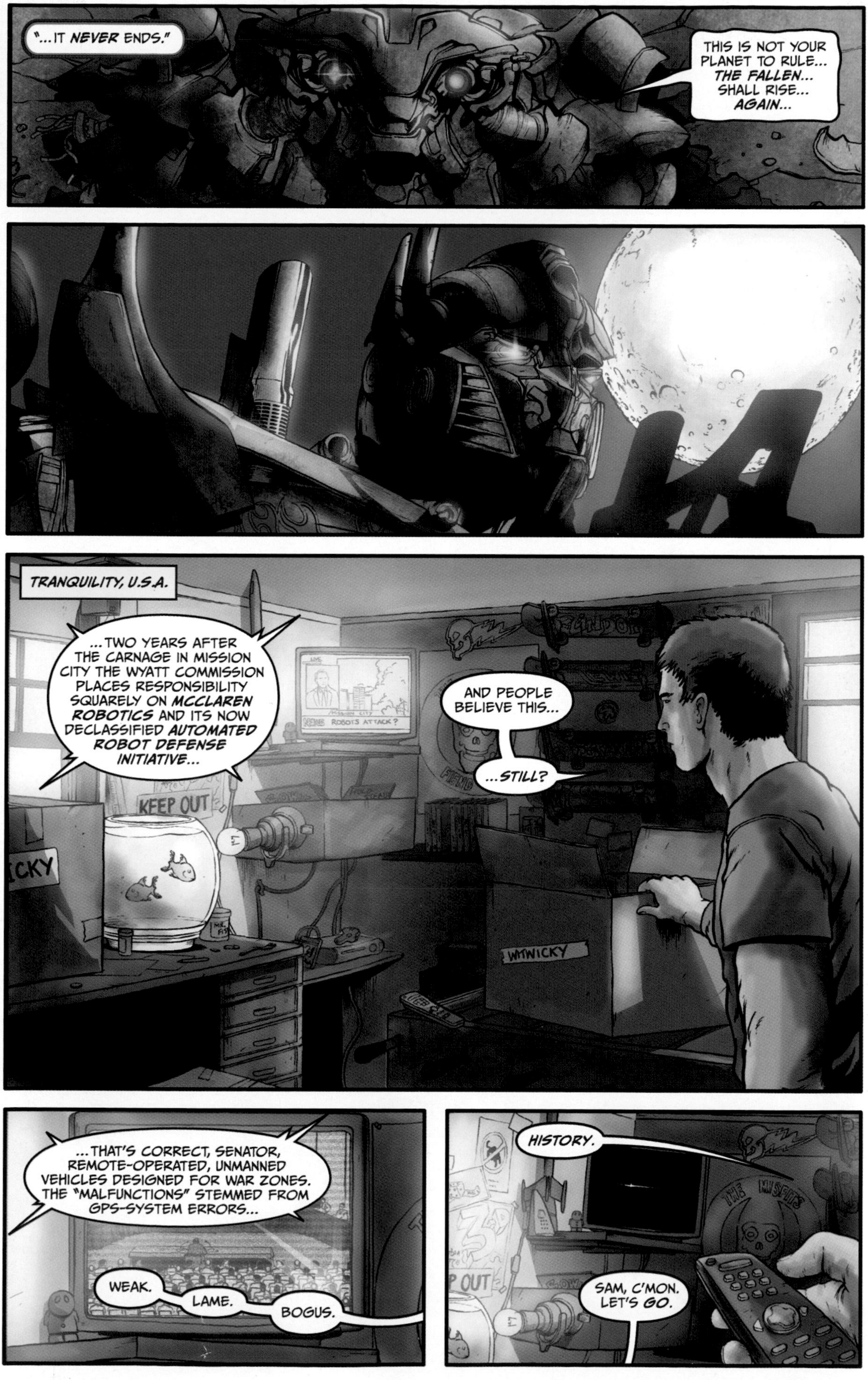
"...IT NEVER ENDS."
THIS IS NOT YOUR PLANET TO RULE... THE FALLEN... SHALL RISE... AGAIN...
TRANQUILITY, U.S.A.
...TWO YEARS AFTER THE CARNAGE IN MISSION CITY THE WYATT COMMISSION PLACES RESPONSIBILITY SQUARELY ON MCCLAREN ROBOTICS AND ITS NOW DECLASSIFIED AUTOMATED ROBOT DEFENSE INITIATIVE...
NEWS ROBOTS ATTACK?
AND PEOPLE BELIEVE THIS...
...STILL?
KEEP OUT
WITWICKY
...THAT'S CORRECT, SENATOR, REMOTE-OPERATED, UNMANNED VEHICLES DESIGNED FOR WAR ZONES. THE "MALFUNCTIONS" STEMMED FROM GPS-SYSTEM ERRORS...
WEAK.
LAME.
BOGUS.
HISTORY.
SAM, C'MON. LET'S GO.

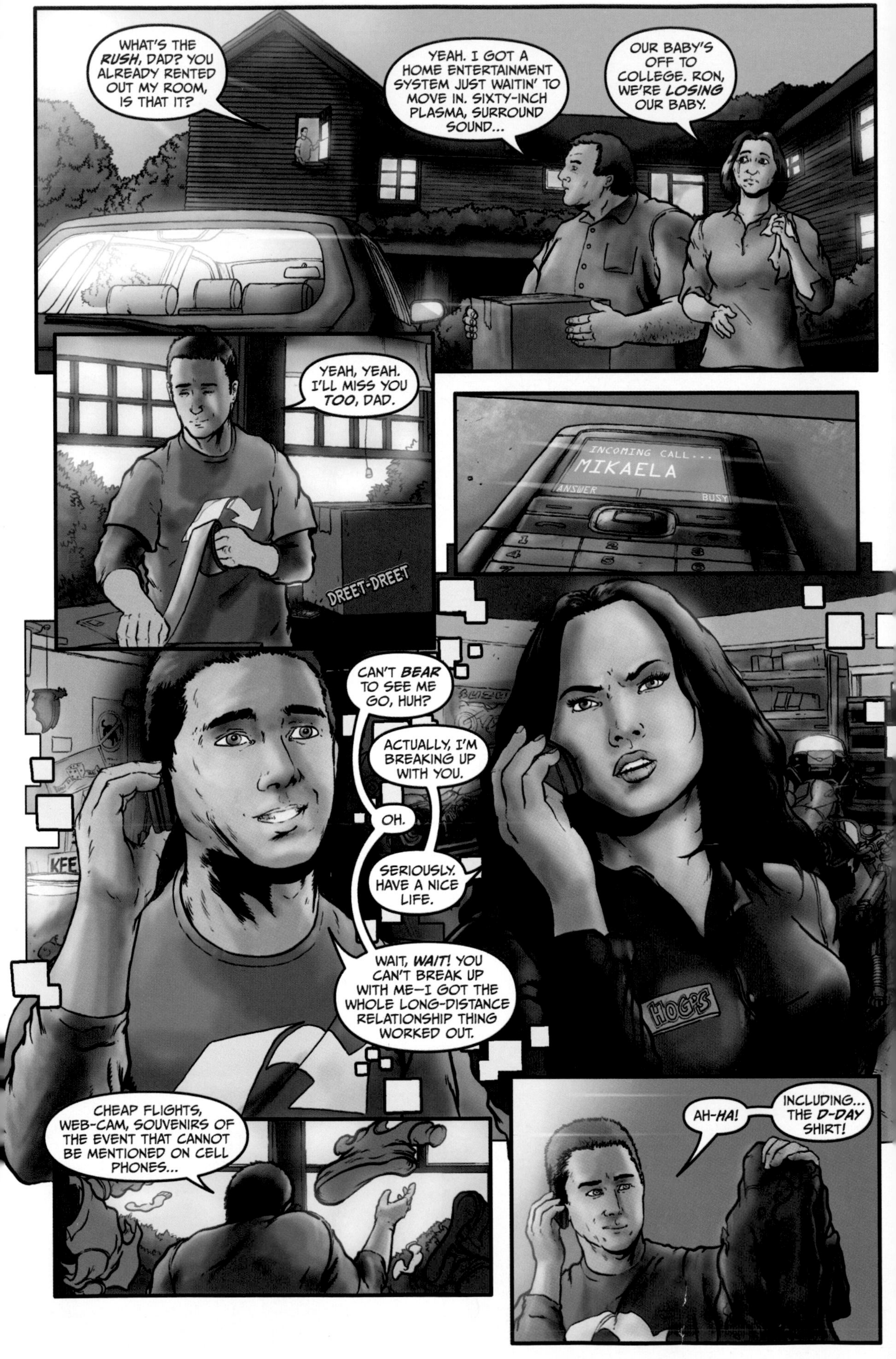
WHAT'S THE RUSH, DAD? YOU ALREADY RENTED OUT MY ROOM, IS THAT IT?
YEAH. I GOT A HOME ENTERTAINMENT SYSTEM JUST WAITIN' TO MOVE IN. SIXTY-INCH PLASMA, SURROUND SOUND...
OUR BABY'S OFF TO COLLEGE. RON, WE'RE LOSING OUR BABY.
YEAH, YEAH. I'LL MISS YOU TOO, DAD.
DREET-DREET
INCOMING CALL...
MIKAELA
ANSWER
BUSY
CAN'T BEAR TO SEE ME GO, HUH?
ACTUALLY, I'M BREAKING UP WITH YOU.
OH.
SERIOUSLY. HAVE A NICE LIFE.
WAIT, WAIT! YOU CAN'T BREAK UP WITH ME—I GOT THE WHOLE LONG-DISTANCE RELATIONSHIP THING WORKED OUT.
HOGPS
CHEAP FLIGHTS, WEB-CAM, SOUVENIRS OF THE EVENT THAT CANNOT BE MENTIONED ON CELL PHONES...
AH-HA!
INCLUDING... THE D-DAY SHIRT!

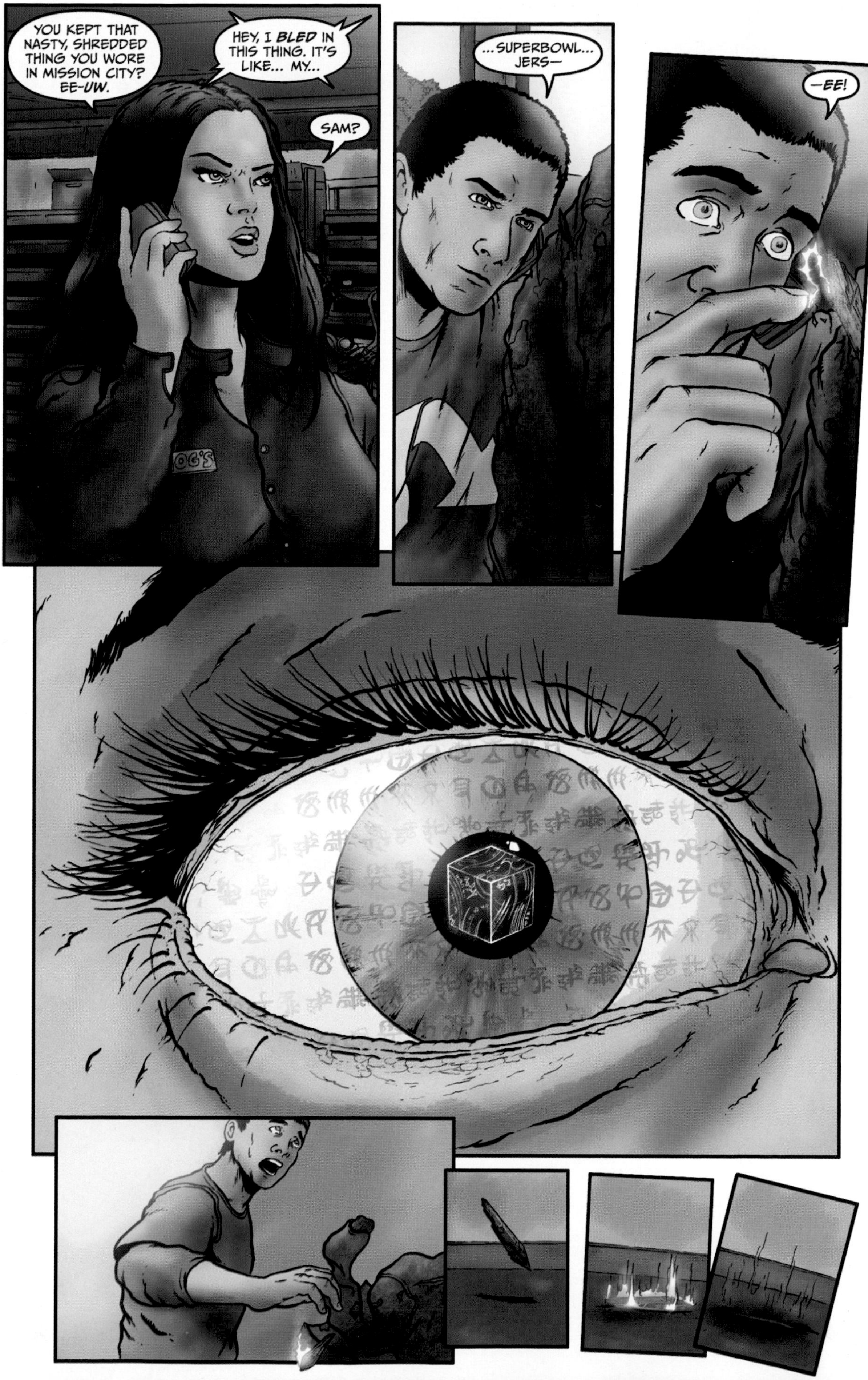
YOU KEPT THAT NASTY, SHREDDED THING YOU WORE IN MISSION CITY? EE-UW.
HEY, I BLED IN THIS THING. IT'S LIKE... MY...
SAM?
...SUPERBOWL... JERS—
—EE!

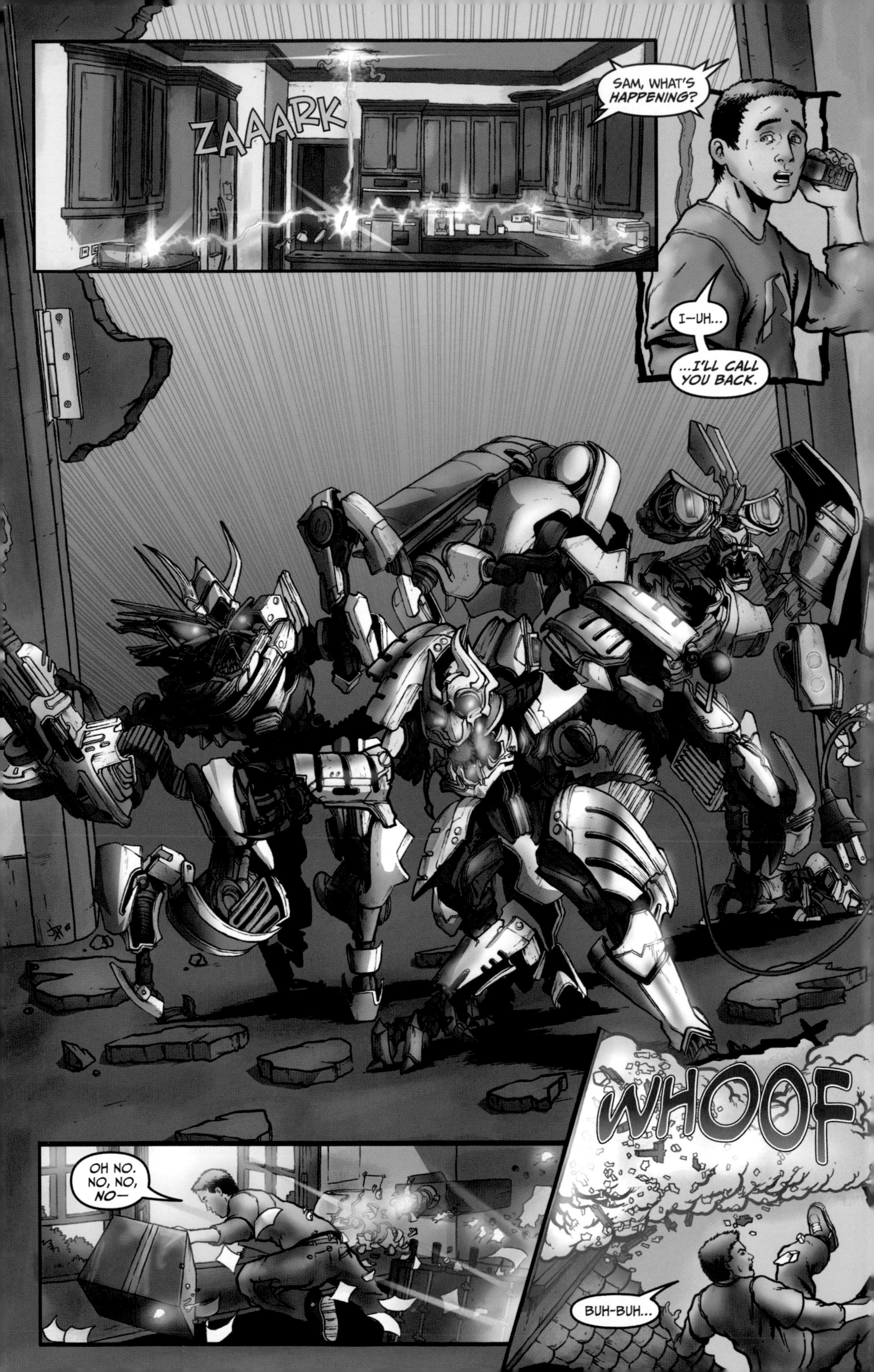
ZAAARK
SAM, WHAT'S HAPPENING?
I—UH...
...I'LL CALL YOU BACK.
WHOOF
OH NO. NO, NO, NO—
BUH-BUH...

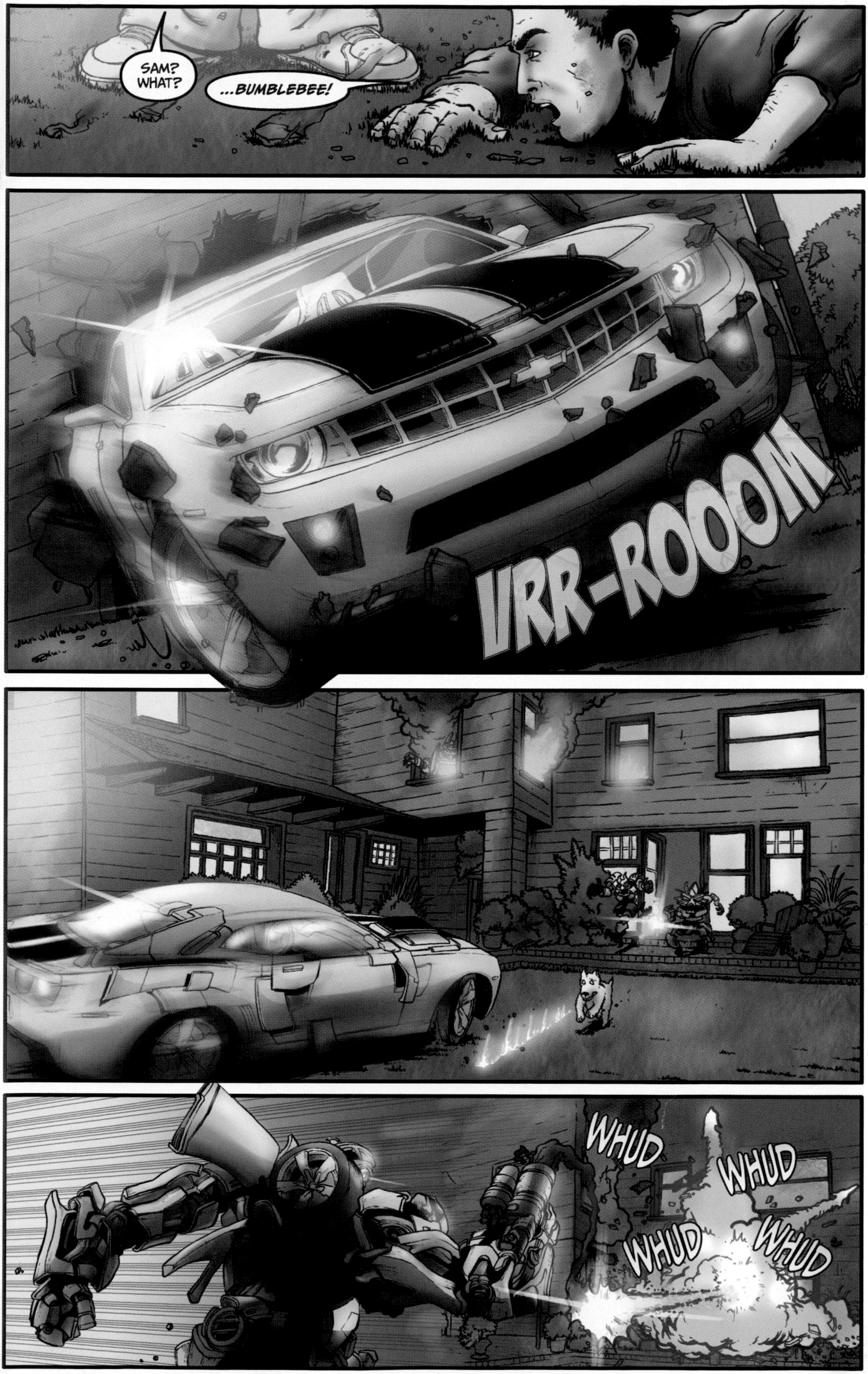
SAM? WHAT?
...BUMBLEBEE!
VRR-ROOOM
WHUD
WHUD
WHUD
WHUD

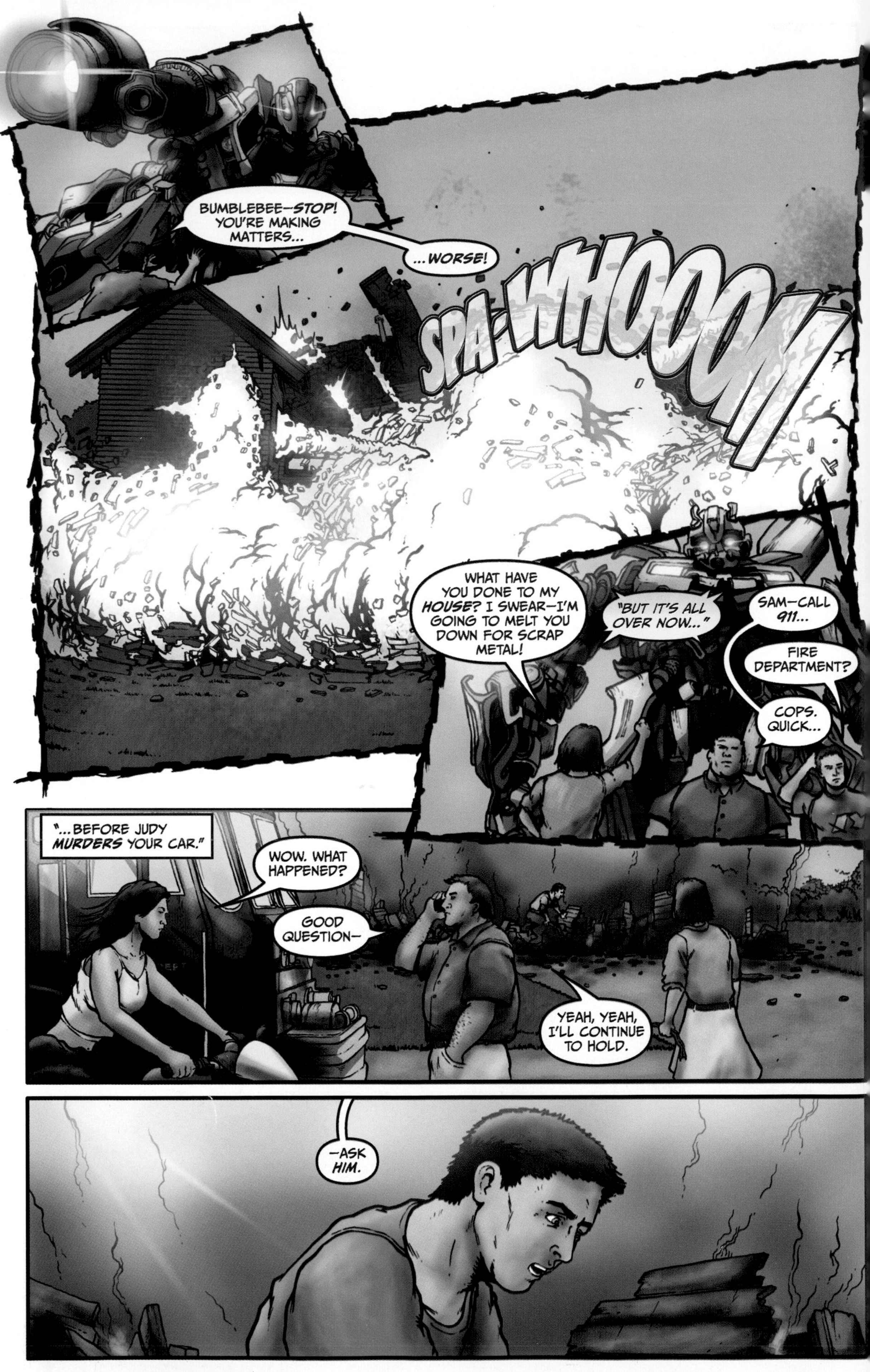
BUMBLEBEE—STOP! YOU'RE MAKING MATTERS...
...WORSE!
SPA-WHOOOM
WHAT HAVE YOU DONE TO MY HOUSE? I SWEAR—I'M GOING TO MELT YOU DOWN FOR SCRAP METAL!
"BUT IT'S ALL OVER NOW..."
SAM—CALL 911...
FIRE DEPARTMENT?
COPS. QUICK...
"...BEFORE JUDY MURDERS YOUR CAR."
WOW. WHAT HAPPENED?
GOOD QUESTION—
YEAH, YEAH, I'LL CONTINUE TO HOLD.
—ASK HIM.

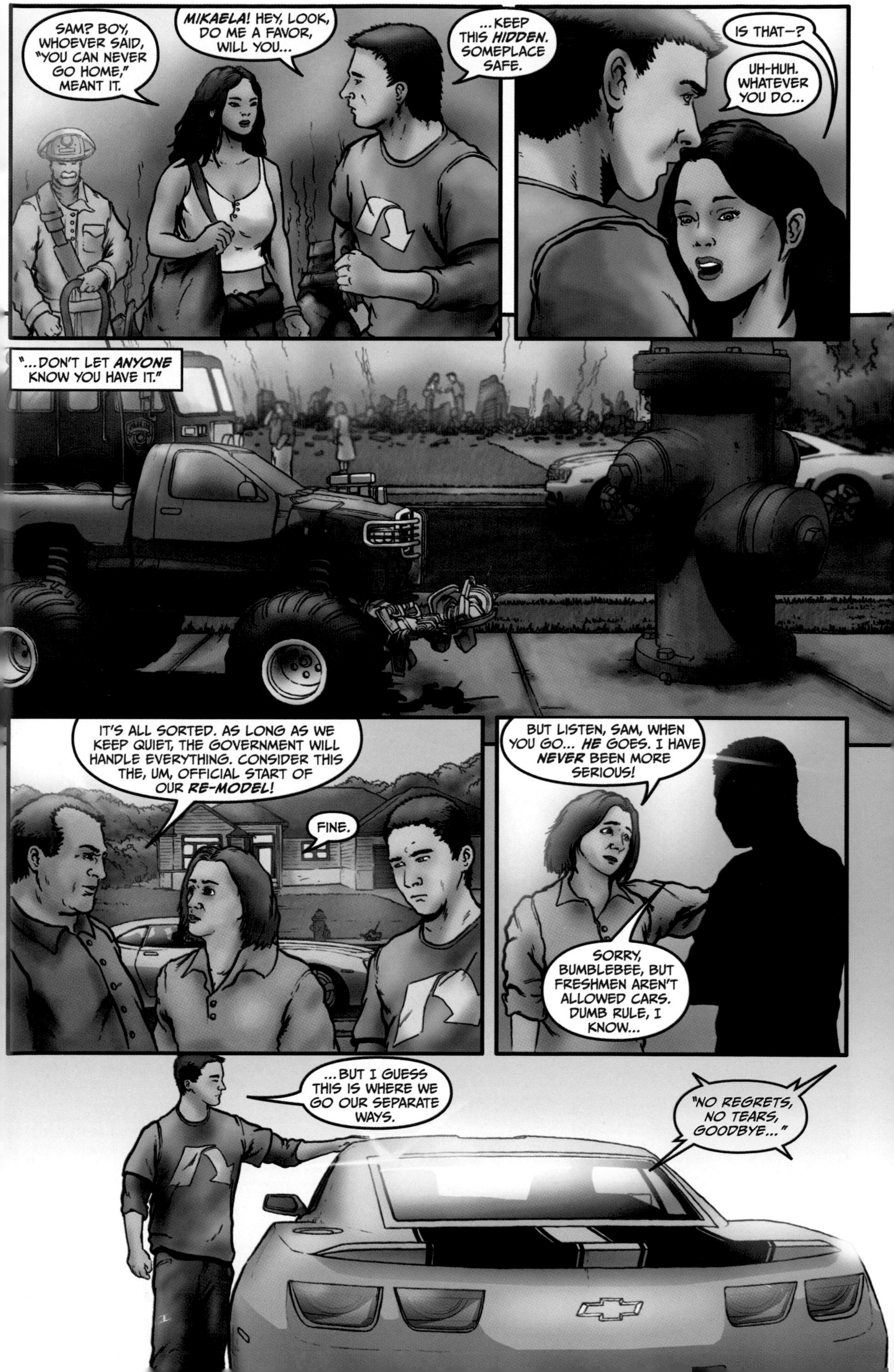
SAM? BOY, WHOEVER SAID, "YOU CAN NEVER GO HOME," MEANT IT.
MIKAELA! HEY, LOOK, DO ME A FAVOR, WILL YOU...
...KEEP THIS HIDDEN. SOMEPLACE SAFE.
IS THAT—?
UH-HUH. WHATEVER YOU DO...
"...DON'T LET ANYONE KNOW YOU HAVE IT."
IT'S ALL SORTED. AS LONG AS WE KEEP QUIET, THE GOVERNMENT WILL HANDLE EVERYTHING. CONSIDER THIS THE, UM, OFFICIAL START OF OUR RE-MODEL!
FINE.
BUT LISTEN, SAM, WHEN YOU GO... HE GOES. I HAVE NEVER BEEN MORE SERIOUS!
SORRY, BUMBLEBEE, BUT FRESHMEN AREN'T ALLOWED CARS. DUMB RULE, I KNOW...
...BUT I GUESS THIS IS WHERE WE GO OUR SEPARATE WAYS.
"NO REGRETS, NO TEARS, GOODBYE..."

DIEGO GARCIA, THE INDIAN OCEAN.

DIRECTOR GALLOWAY, HONOR TO HAVE YOU ON SITE. BUT... I'M AFRAID YOU'RE *NOT* ON THE ACCESS LIST.

I AM NOW.

PRESIDENTIAL ORDER, MAJOR. MY MESSAGE...

"...IS FOR YOUR *CLASSIFIED* SPACE BUDDIES."

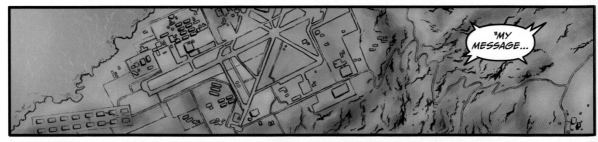

"MY MESSAGE...

"...IS FOR YOUR *CLASSIFIED* SPACE BUDDIES."

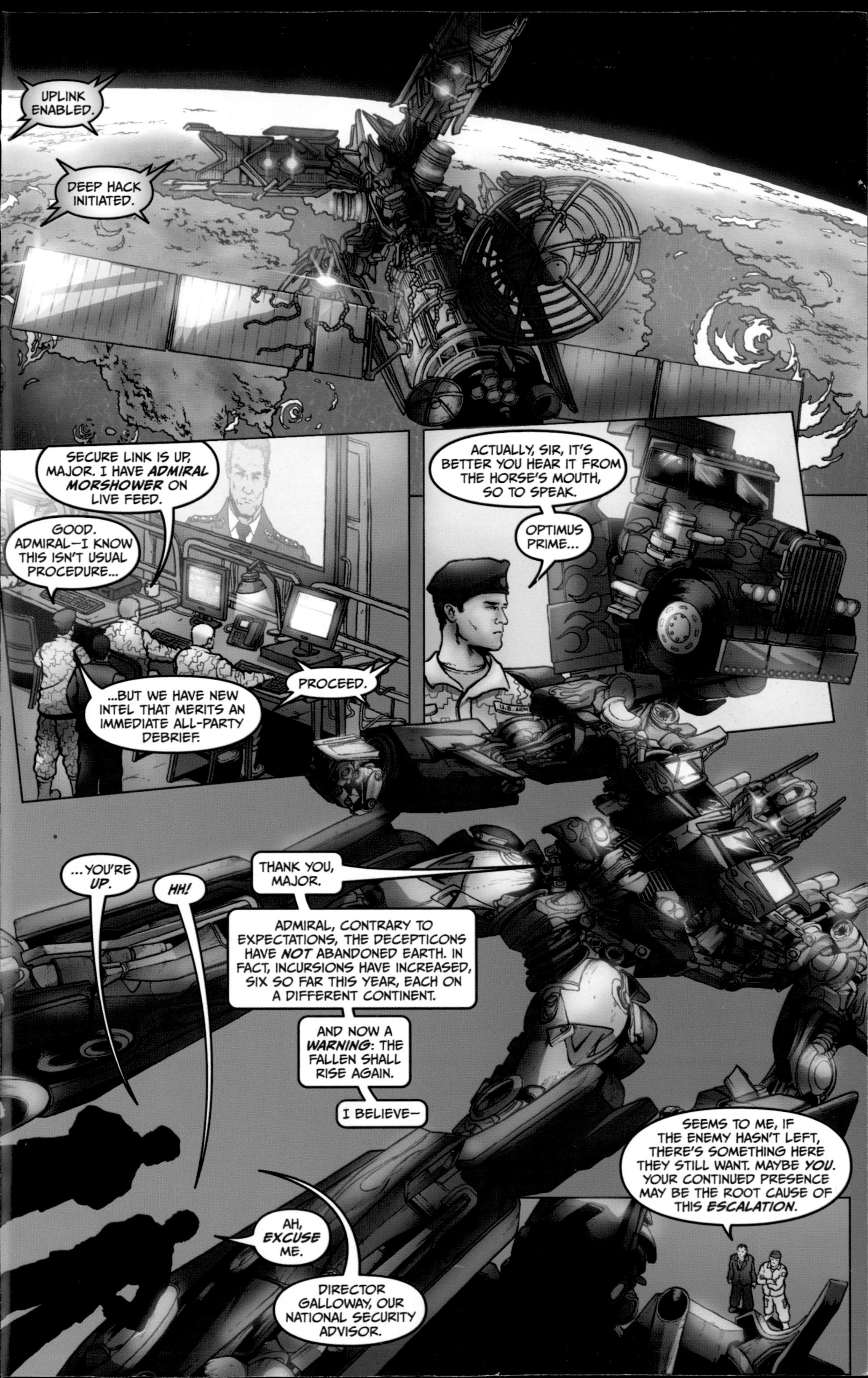
UPLINK ENABLED.
DEEP HACK INITIATED.
SECURE LINK IS UP, MAJOR. I HAVE ADMIRAL MORSHOWER ON LIVE FEED.
GOOD. ADMIRAL—I KNOW THIS ISN'T USUAL PROCEDURE...
...BUT WE HAVE NEW INTEL THAT MERITS AN IMMEDIATE ALL-PARTY DEBRIEF.
PROCEED.
ACTUALLY, SIR, IT'S BETTER YOU HEAR IT FROM THE HORSE'S MOUTH, SO TO SPEAK.
OPTIMUS PRIME...
U.S. ARMY
...YOU'RE UP.
HH!
THANK YOU, MAJOR.
ADMIRAL, CONTRARY TO EXPECTATIONS, THE DECEPTICONS HAVE NOT ABANDONED EARTH. IN FACT, INCURSIONS HAVE INCREASED, SIX SO FAR THIS YEAR, EACH ON A DIFFERENT CONTINENT.
AND NOW A WARNING: THE FALLEN SHALL RISE AGAIN.
I BELIEVE—
AH, EXCUSE ME.
DIRECTOR GALLOWAY, OUR NATIONAL SECURITY ADVISOR.
SEEMS TO ME, IF THE ENEMY HASN'T LEFT, THERE'S SOMETHING HERE THEY STILL WANT. MAYBE YOU. YOUR CONTINUED PRESENCE MAY BE THE ROOT CAUSE OF THIS ESCALATION.

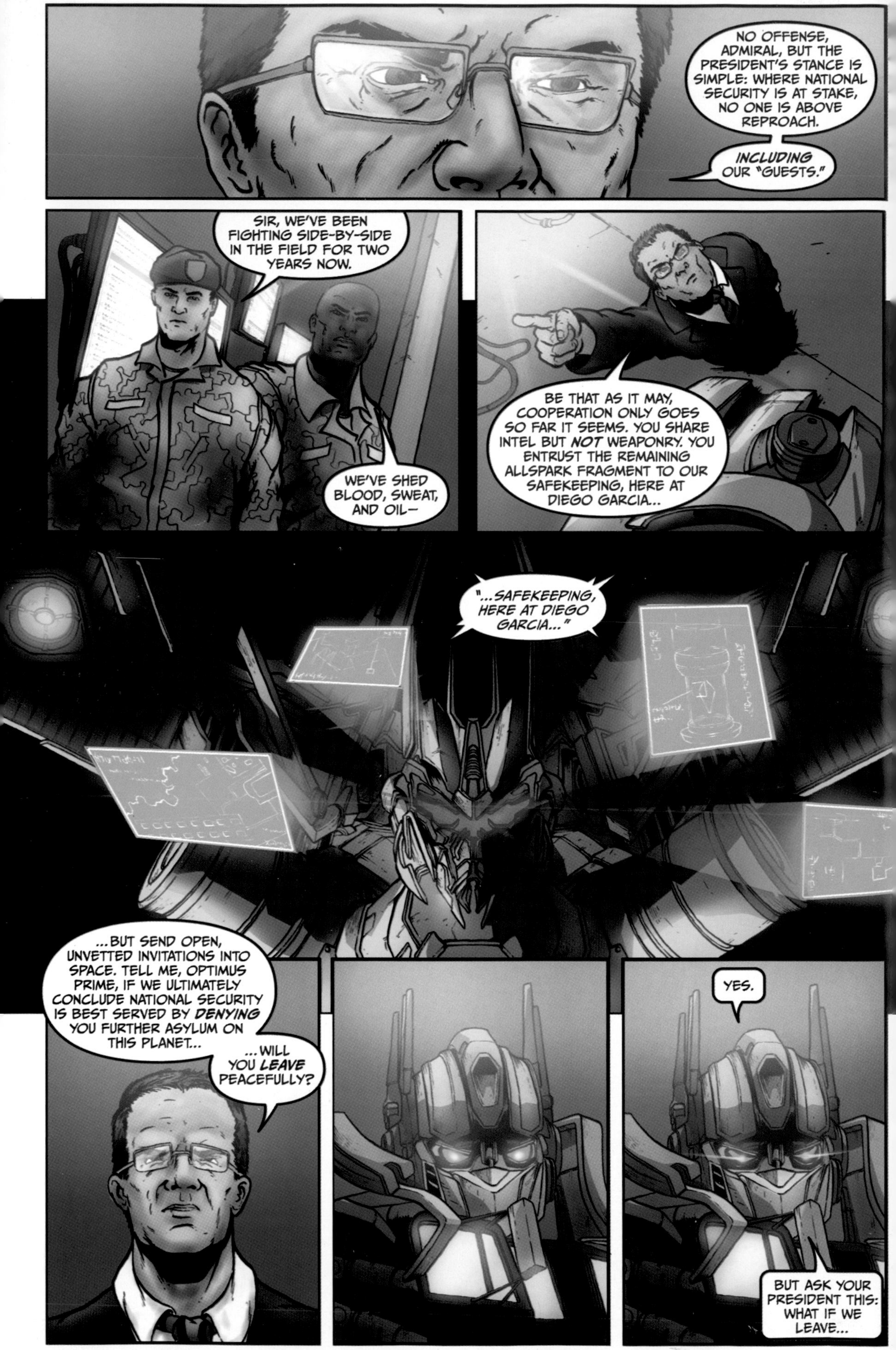
NO OFFENSE, ADMIRAL, BUT THE PRESIDENT'S STANCE IS SIMPLE: WHERE NATIONAL SECURITY IS AT STAKE, NO ONE IS ABOVE REPROACH.
INCLUDING OUR "GUESTS."
SIR, WE'VE BEEN FIGHTING SIDE-BY-SIDE IN THE FIELD FOR TWO YEARS NOW.
WE'VE SHED BLOOD, SWEAT, AND OIL—
BE THAT AS IT MAY, COOPERATION ONLY GOES SO FAR IT SEEMS. YOU SHARE INTEL BUT *NOT* WEAPONRY. YOU ENTRUST THE REMAINING ALLSPARK FRAGMENT TO OUR SAFEKEEPING, HERE AT DIEGO GARCIA...
"...SAFEKEEPING, HERE AT DIEGO GARCIA..."
...BUT SEND OPEN, UNVETTED INVITATIONS INTO SPACE. TELL ME, OPTIMUS PRIME, IF WE ULTIMATELY CONCLUDE NATIONAL SECURITY IS BEST SERVED BY *DENYING* YOU FURTHER ASYLUM ON THIS PLANET...
...WILL YOU *LEAVE* PEACEFULLY?
YES.
BUT ASK YOUR PRESIDENT THIS: WHAT IF WE LEAVE...

"...AND YOU'RE **WRONG**?"

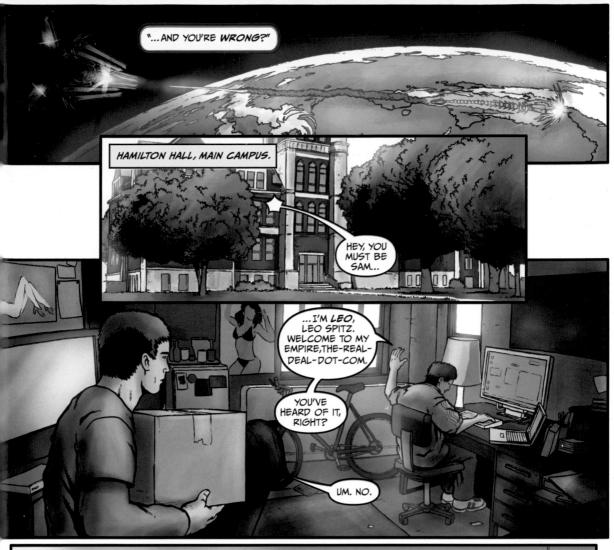

HAMILTON HALL, MAIN CAMPUS.

HEY, YOU MUST BE SAM...

...I'M *LEO*, LEO SPITZ. WELCOME TO MY EMPIRE, THE-REAL-DEAL-DOT-COM.

YOU'VE HEARD OF IT, RIGHT?

UM. NO.

http://www.bigeffingrobots.com/ch

soundofbots

File Edit Bytes Tools

SHARSKY

chinarobotsmash

POST IT—*GO, GO!* F.T.J., BABY!

HEY, LEO, WE GOT SOME BRAND NEW SHANGHAI VID.

F.T.J.?

FASSBINDER

FUEL THE JET!

YOU SEE THIS? HALF OF SHANGHAI GETS WRECKED AND CHINA SAYS "GAS LEAK"? YEAH, *RIGHT.*

LEO, BAD NEWS. WE GOT SCOOPED: THE VID'S ALREADY UP ON G.F.R.

G.F.R.?

GIANT-ROBOTS-DOT-COM. OUR MAIN COMPETITION. RUN BY SOMEONE CALLING HIMSELF "ROBO-WARRIOR."

Y'KNOW, MAYBE I'LL SEE IF THERE ARE ANY *OTHER* ROOMS AVAILABLE—

UH, HI THERE! SAM? I'M *ALICE!*

LOOKS LIKE WE'RE NEIGHBORS...

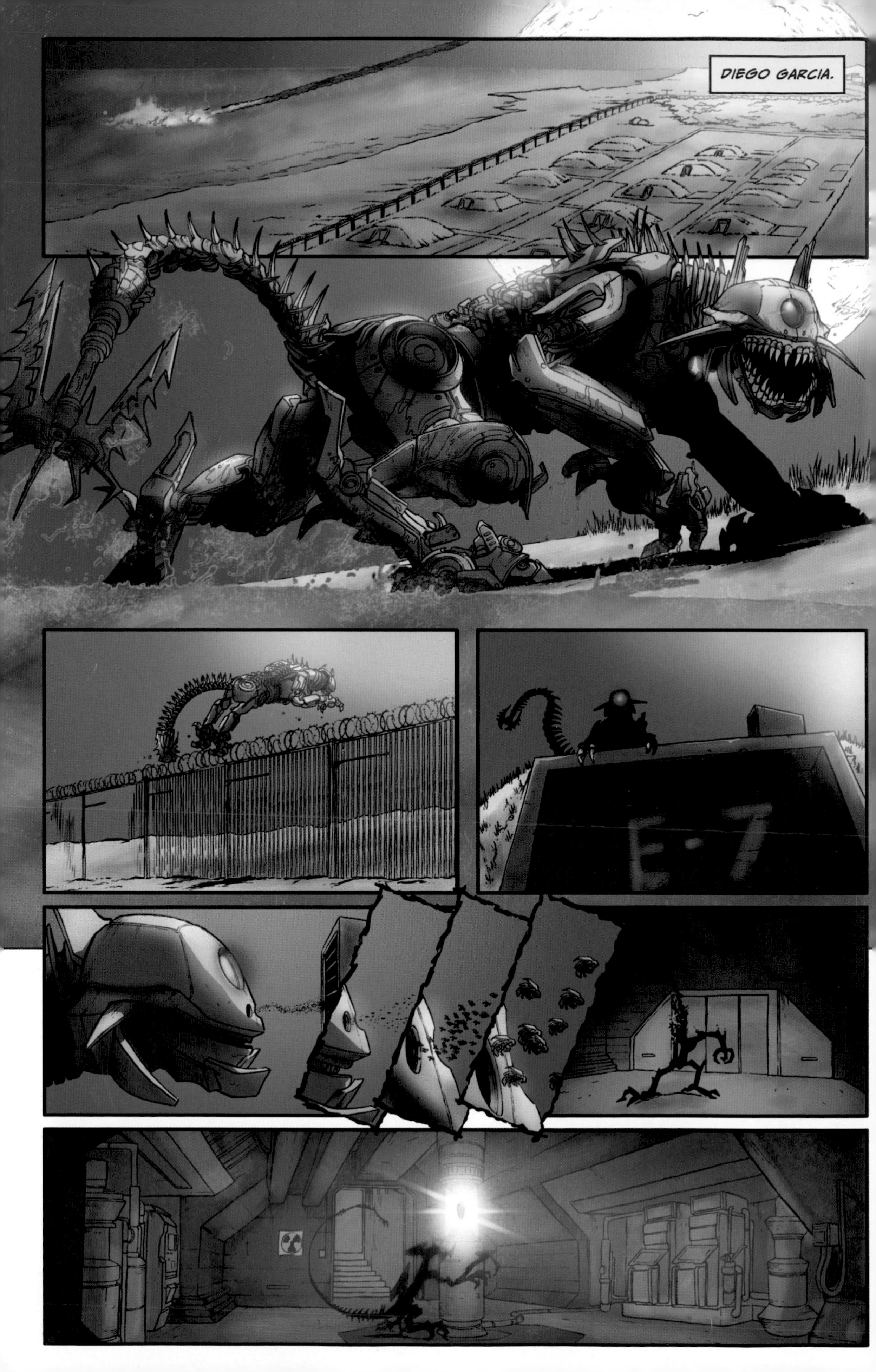
DIEGO GARCIA.
E-7

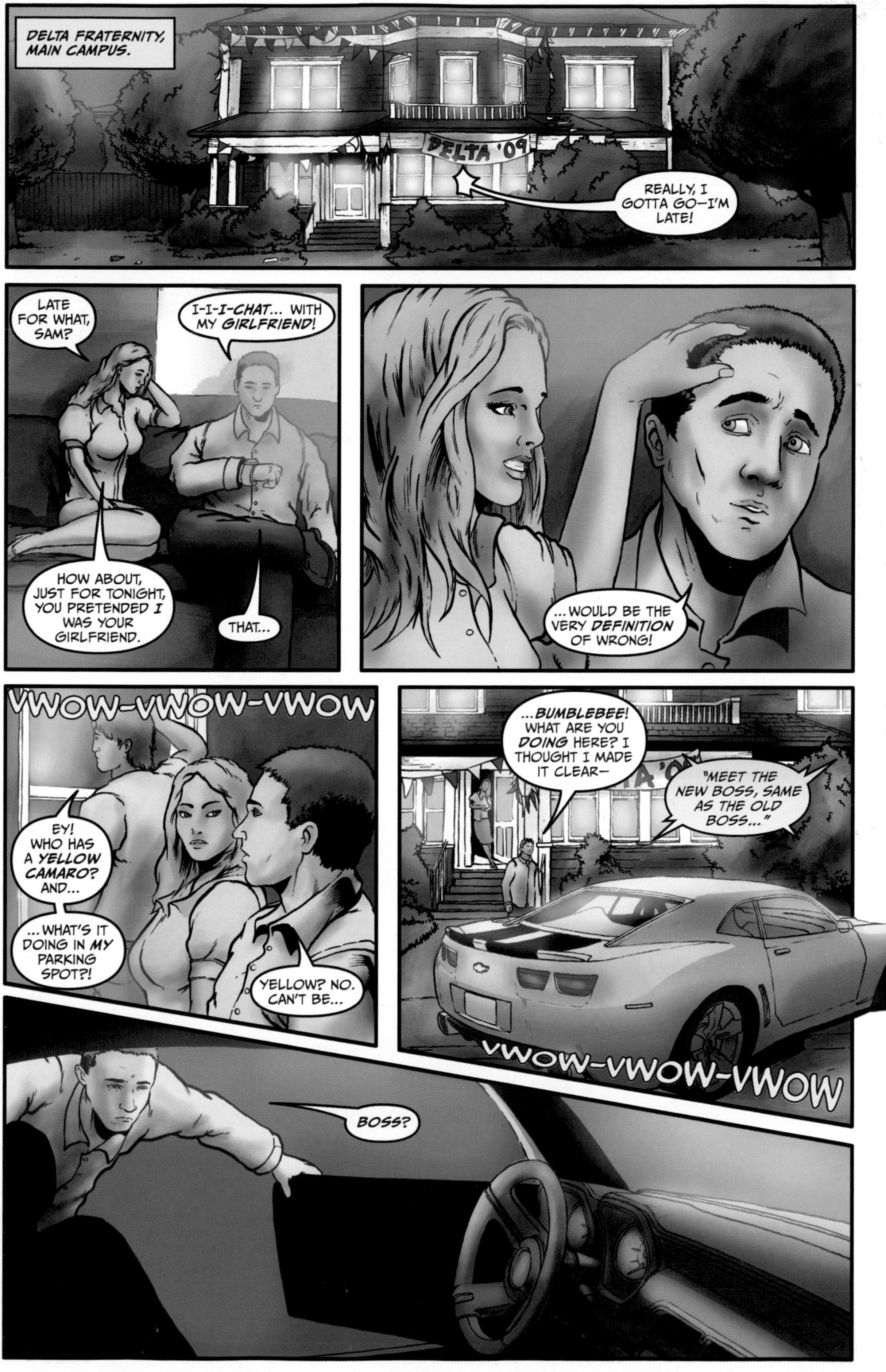
DELTA FRATERNITY, MAIN CAMPUS.
DELTA '09
REALLY, I GOTTA GO—I'M LATE!
LATE FOR WHAT, SAM?
I-I-I-CHAT... WITH MY GIRLFRIEND!
HOW ABOUT, JUST FOR TONIGHT, YOU PRETENDED I WAS YOUR GIRLFRIEND.
THAT...
...WOULD BE THE VERY DEFINITION OF WRONG!
VWOW-VWOW-VWOW
EY! WHO HAS A YELLOW CAMARO? AND...
...WHAT'S IT DOING IN MY PARKING SPOT?!
YELLOW? NO. CAN'T BE...
...BUMBLEBEE! WHAT ARE YOU DOING HERE? I THOUGHT I MADE IT CLEAR—
"MEET THE NEW BOSS, SAME AS THE OLD BOSS..."
VWOW-VWOW-VWOW
BOSS?

THANK YOU FOR COMING, SAM.

WE ARE ONCE MORE IN NEED OF YOUR HELP.

HELP? I THOUGHT YOU GUYS AND THE POWERS-THAT-BE WERE ALL ONE BIG, HAPPY FAMILY.

IT'S ALL CHANGED, SAM.

SOME OF YOUR LEADERS BELIEVE WE HAVE BROUGHT *VENGEANCE* UPON THIS WORLD. AND NOW, THE ALLSPARK FRAGMENT WE PLACED UNDER HUMAN PROTECTION...

"...HAS BEEN *STOLEN*."

NORTH ATLANTIC OCEAN.

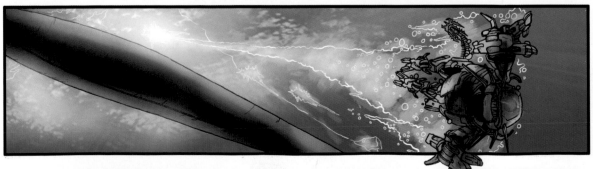

I JUST... DON'T SEE WHAT I CAN DO.

SPEAK *FOR* US, STAND *WITH* US.

LOOK, I'M SORRY, I'M JUST *NOT* THIS GUY YOU WANT ME TO BE. THIS *ISN'T* MY WAR.

SAM, YOUR ONLY SHORTCOMING IS YOUR OWN LACK OF INSIGHT. YOU ARE MORE THAN—

NO!

LISTEN! I'M AN AVERAGE STUDENT, A BELOW-PAR ATHLETE, AND AN OKAY HUMAN BEING. NOTHING I DO IS *EVER* GOING TO MAKE A DIFFERENCE.

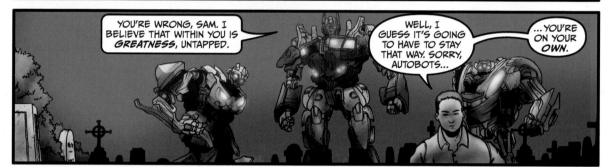

YOU'RE WRONG, SAM. I BELIEVE THAT WITHIN YOU IS *GREATNESS*, UNTAPPED.

WELL, I GUESS IT'S GOING TO HAVE TO STAY THAT WAY. SORRY, AUTOBOTS...

...YOU'RE ON YOUR *OWN*.

RAVAGE, THE SHARD.

I HAVE DONE ALL I CAN. WE GO...

...BEYOND SCIENCE.

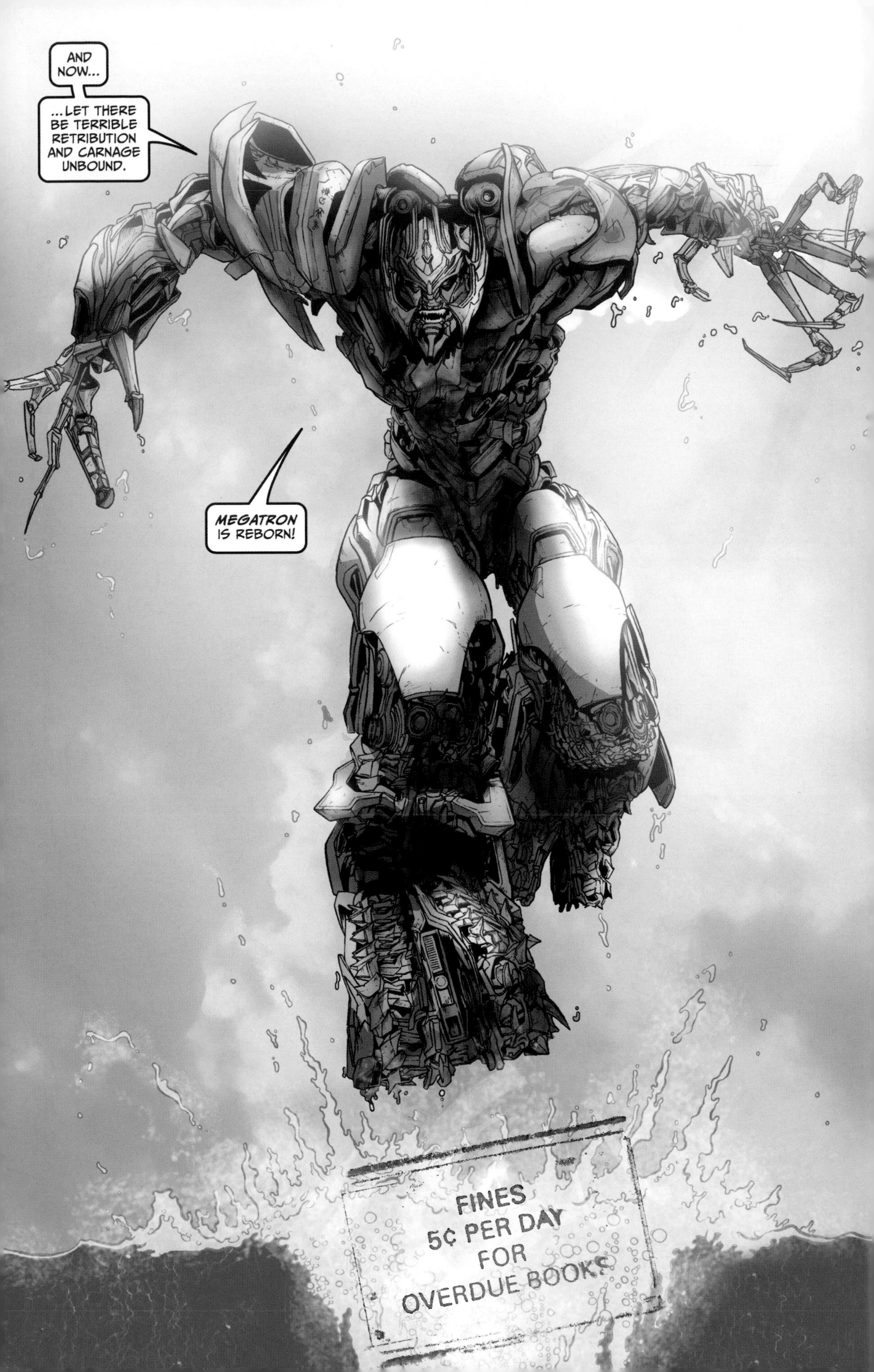
AND NOW...
...LET THERE BE TERRIBLE RETRIBUTION AND CARNAGE UNBOUND.
MEGATRON IS REBORN!
FINES 5¢ PER DAY FOR OVERDUE BOOKS